THE SUGAR-GUM TREE

PATRICIA WRIGHTSON

THE SUGAR-GUM TREE

Illustrated by
DAVID COX

VIKING

Viking
Penguin Books Australia Ltd
487 Maroondah Highway, PO Box 257
Ringwood, Victoria 3134, Australia
Penguin Books Ltd
Harmondsworth, Middlesex, England
Viking Penguin, A Division of Penguin Books USA Inc.
375 Hudson Street, New York, New York 10014, USA
Penguin Books Canada Limited
10 Alcorn Avenue, Toronto, Ontario, Canada M4V 1E4
Penguin Books (N.Z.) Ltd
182-190 Wairau Road, Auckland 10, New Zealand

First published by Penguin Books Australia, 1991
10 9 8 7 6 5 4 3 2 1
Copyright © Patricia Wrightson, 1991
Illustrations Copyright © David Cox, 1991

Typeset in Bembo by Leader Composition
Made and printed in Australia by Australian Print Group, Maryborough, Vic.

National Library of Australia
Cataloguing-in-Publication data:

Wrightson, Patricia, 1921-
The sugar-gum tree.

ISBN 0 670 83910 8.

I. Cox, David, 1933- .II. Title.

A823.3

Sarah Bell and Penny May were best friends. They both played in the Bells' yard, or they both played in the Mays' yard.

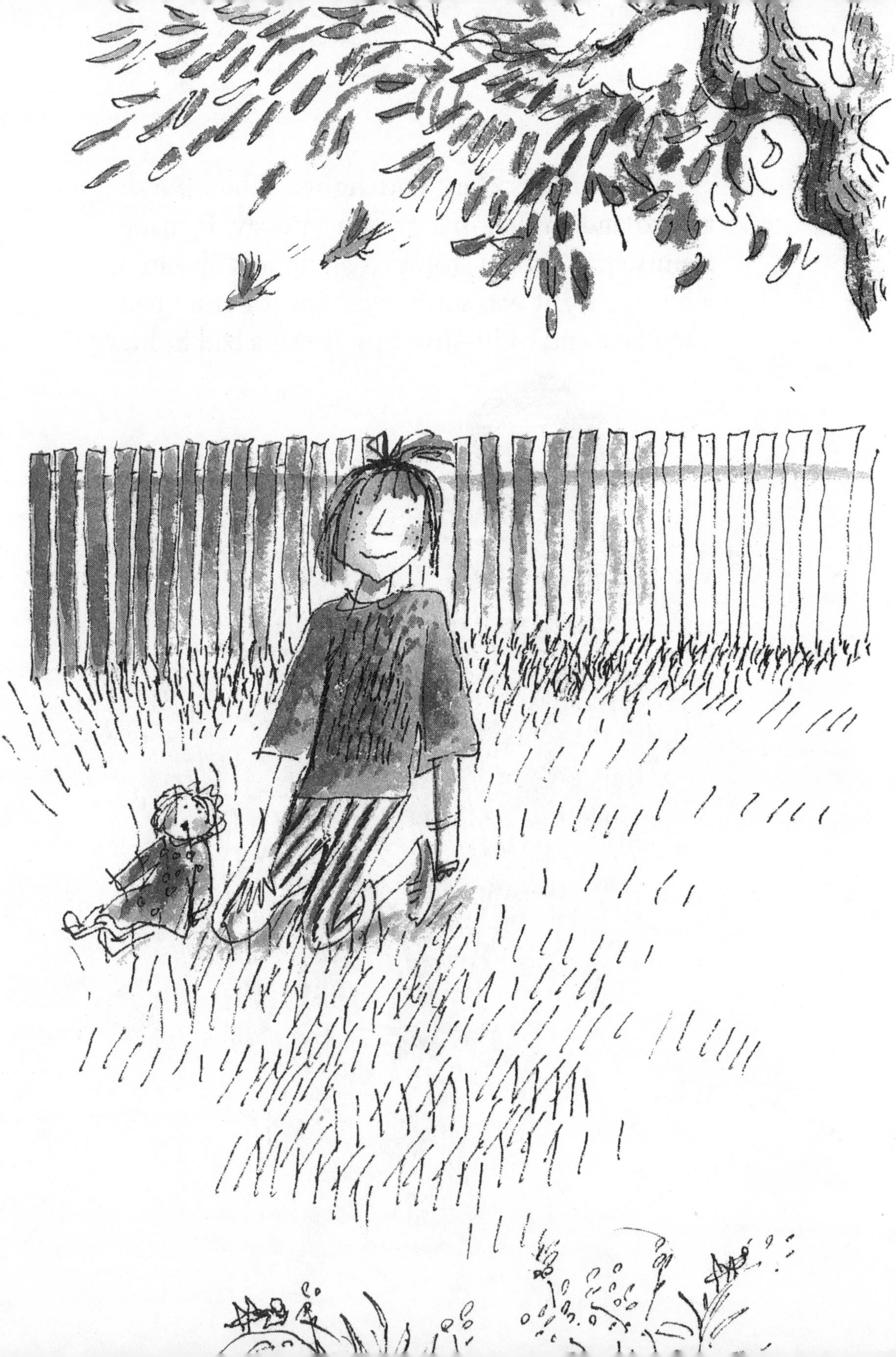

Sometimes they had fights. Then Sarah talked and smiled in a grown-up way. It made Penny mad. If she stomped about and shouted a bit, the fight was soon over; but if Penny had a red face and tight-shut lips, it was a bad fight.

After the fights they were best friends
again.

Sarah was making a house, under the sugar-gum tree in her back yard. Penny came round to help. There was a lot of stuff lying around the tree. Penny had a good look.

'Where did the rug come from?' she asked.

'The tip,' Sarah told her. 'When dad took me. It's clean, even. Mum helped me.'

'It's magic. What are the bricks for?'

'The stove, I think. Or it could be chairs.'

'There's a lot. You can have a little stove and two chairs.'

Sarah frowned; she hadn't made up her mind. She said, 'The stove has to fit the pan mum gave me.'

Penny went to look at the pan. 'Cups too!' she cried. 'Your mother gave you cups!'

'Only two,' said Sarah. 'And they're cracked.'

'I was going to bring my old teaset!'

'You still can,' said Sarah quickly, because she could tell that Penny was hurt. 'We need more cups and there's no teapot.'

'You know my teapot's broken,' Penny said in a grumpy way. She *was* hurt.

The house was made from an old quilt.
Sarah tied it to the tree with string.

'That needs a nail,' said Penny. She was
good with nails. She went into Mr Bell's shed,
and came back with a hammer and a nail.

'Oh, Penny!' cried Sarah. 'You can't put a nail in dad's good sugar-gum tree!' Sarah was good with string, and it was her house.

'If a wind comes,' said Penny, 'the whole house could blow away.'

She stood on an apple-crate and nailed the quilt to the tree.

'Now you've made the house crooked,' Sarah told her crossly.

Penny reached up to pull the quilt straight. There was a loud, cracking noise, and she tumbled down. The thin wood of the apple-crate had broken.

'Look what you've done!' cried Sarah. 'That was my table! Penny May, you're a gloop!'

Penny stood up slowly. She was frowning, and there was a long, red scratch on her leg. She said, 'That's not very nice. Calling people a . . .'

'A gloop,' said Sarah, helping in a grown-up way.

' . . . when they've fallen down and hurt their leg and they're only trying to help. You ought to say sorry.'

'Me?' said Sarah, smiling her grown-up smile. '*You* ought to say sorry. Putting nails into dad's tree and breaking my table. Go on. Say you're sorry.'

Penny shut her lips tight. Her face went red. She jumped at a branch of the sugar-gum tree, pulled herself up and began to climb.

'Come down!' Sarah called, but Penny went on climbing. 'You're just being another gloop!' cried Sarah.

Penny climbed quite high. Then she sat
in the fork of a branch and shouted angrily:
'I won't come down till you say you're
sorry!'

Sarah was upset; but of course she wasn't sorry. It was her house, and people should make their house their own way. It wasn't fair for Sarah to say sorry when Penny was the one to blame. But when would Penny come down from the tree?

Sarah didn't know what to do, so she went on making the house. Penny went on sitting in the tree. She didn't even look down, but stared away over all the back yards.

Sarah put the old rug into the house for a
floor. She carried bricks in, and made a stove
and two chairs. She turned the apple-crate over
to hide the broken part, and put it in the place
for a table. She put the cups on the table and
the pan on the stove.

Penny was still sitting in the tree.

'I think that looks nice,' said Sarah. She said it to herself but loudly, in case Penny wanted to come down and look. 'But there ought to be flowers.' She went to the geraniums under her bedroom window, and picked some flowers. She put them in a cup on the table.

Penny stared away at the back yards.

'It's nearly dinner-time,' said Sarah, to herself but loudly. 'Dad will be home soon.' She waited for a bit, but nothing happened.

Sarah went slowly to the back door. Maybe her mother could sort things out.

Mrs Bell was in the kitchen. She said, 'You're in early. Has Penny gone home?'

'No,' said Sarah, not looking at anything.

'Where is she, then?'

'In the sugar-gum tree,' said Sarah.

Mrs Bell dropped a potato. 'Sarah, that tree isn't safe. You've both been told that the branches often break.'

'I know,' said Sarah. 'She won't come down.'

'Oh, Sarah, not another fight!' Mrs Bell dried her hands. 'You come with me, young lady.' She marched out to the sugar-gum tree, with Sarah trailing behind.

'Penny!' called Mrs Bell. 'Be careful of that tree, dear! Its branches break quite easily. You'd better come down now, anyway. It's nearly dinner-time.'

Penny's face got red again. 'Sarah's got to say sorry. She called me a . . .'

'A gloop,' said Sarah in a small voice.

'She's got to say sorry,' called Penny, hugging the tree in case its branch broke.

'SARAH,' said Mrs Bell sternly.

'I'm sorry,' whispered Sarah, though she knew it wasn't fair.

'Say it louder. She's right up the tree.'

Sarah put her head back and shouted. 'I'M SORRY!' Then she added, just moving her lips and making no sound, 'That Penny May is such a gloop.'

'She said it again!' shouted Penny. 'I saw her! She called me it again!'

'Sarah,' said Mrs Bell, 'go to your room and stay there. Penny May, I'm going to ring up your mother. She'll be home from work by now.'

Sarah slumped off to her room. She could hear Mrs Bell ringing up Mrs May. She sat on her bed and stared glumly out of the window. There was the quilt-house, still a bit crooked. There was Penny, so high that she looked small.

Now her face wasn't red; it was glum, like Sarah's, and she clung tight to the tree. Sarah gave her a little wave. They were both in the same trouble; and it must be awful for Penny, up in the tree by herself with her mother coming.

The car drove into the shed: now dad was home.

He came into the yard, and stopped to look at the quilt-house, shaking his head. He picked up his hammer and put it away.

Then he went inside. He hadn't looked into the tree.

Sarah waited. Mum and dad were talking in the kitchen. After a while, dad came out again.

'Hi, there!' he called into the sugar-gum. 'Are you going to stay and have dinner with Sarah?'

Penny shook her head. She couldn't talk now, even if she tried.

'It's not very nice,' called Mr Bell, 'spending the night in a tree. What if you go to sleep? Will you fall?'

Penny looked as if she might cry.

'Don't you want to get down before your mother comes?' called Mr Bell. 'We can all have a Coke while we wait.'

Penny shook her head again. Mr Bell came over to look at the geraniums. Then he looked through the window, at Sarah.

'You know you're a brat, don't you?' he
said in a cross voice. 'It's time you got some
sense.'

Sarah didn't tell him it wasn't fair,
because now she couldn't talk, either. She only
looked at him, and he went inside.

The front door-bell rang, and the house was full of voices: both Mr and Mrs May had come. There was loud talking for a while, and suddenly all the grown-ups spilt out of the back door into the yard.

'Penny!' called Mrs May. 'You come down out of that tree this very minute, do you hear?'

'And stay close to the trunk,' called Mr May.

Penny stared at all the people. Then she screwed up her mouth and shut her eyes.

Mrs Bell called to her, coaxing. 'Penny, dear, I promise nobody is going to be cross. Just come down while it's still daylight, and before you fall. Sarah is going to say she's sorry.'

Penny clung to the tree, and stared away over all the back yards.

'I know what it is,' said Mrs May. 'The child is badly frightened. Penny, dear, can you hear me? Don't be scared, we're all here to help. Come down now if you can; and if you can't, never mind. Just hang on and keep still. Dad will call the Fire Department.'

Sarah felt dreadful. The Fire Department! Oh, no!

'No!' shouted Penny furiously, and shut her mouth tight. Her face was very red.

'For goodness sake!' called Mrs May. 'What *are* we to do, then? You know we can't leave you in a tree all night.'

They waited a minute. The grown-ups talked softly to each other. At last Mr May went inside to call the Fire Department. After that, all the grown-ups stood gazing into the tree.

Soon, from a long way off, came the
howling of a siren. Sarah felt sick. Penny
wound her arms and legs tightly
round the tree. The siren
came nearer, nearer; it was
the loudest sound in the
world. The red fire-engine
came rushing round the corner.
It stopped outside the back fence.

There were four firemen. They talked in loud, kind voices to the grown-ups and to Penny. They put up a ladder, right over the back fence and into the sugar-gum tree.

One man came climbing along the ladder. He kept talking loudly and kindly to Penny. He told her it was all right, she was quite safe, he was coming; and he told her he had a little girl of his own, about her size.

Penny kept her eyes and mouth tightly shut. She gripped the tree with her arms and legs and clung like a koala. The fireman couldn't pull her off.

'That's a good, sensible girl,' he said, 'holding on so tight. But I've got you safe; you can let go now.'

Penny didn't let go. She clung like a koala. The fireman talked and pulled for a long time. Then he went back across the ladder. He told Mr May he was afraid of breaking the tree.

Mrs May was crying. Everyone was worried. All the firemen talked to Mr May and Mr Bell. They said something about a net.

'What for?' said Penny's fireman. 'She's not going to fall.'

The men took the ladder down, and Mr
Bell herded everyone into the house. They
went on talking in a worried way. It was
beginning to get dark.

Sarah pushed her
window wide open. She
put her chair near it,
climbed over the sill,
jumped down into the
geraniums and ran
very fast to the sugar-
gum tree.

'Quick, Penny!'
she shouted. 'Now!
This way, quick!'

Penny came climbing
and tumbling out of
the tree. She reached
the lowest branch and
fell on to Sarah. They
scrambled up and ran
to the window. It was
high, but they jumped
and wriggled and pulled
themselves up. They had to.

At last they were standing in Sarah's room. They stared at each other. They still couldn't believe it. Not the Fire Department!

'What now?' said Penny in a tight, hard voice.

Sarah didn't know what now, but she knew it had to be fast. Mum would come soon. She said, 'We'll get into bed, and serve them right. Here – pyjamas – hurry up!'

Quickly they put on pyjamas and climbed
into Sarah's bed. There were footsteps coming
down the hall. Sarah and Penny lay down and
shut their eyes. They had just fitted themselves
together when the door opened, and Mrs Bell
switched on the light.

She didn't say a word. She just looked for
a while and went away.

Sarah and Penny stayed as they were.
They didn't know what else to do.

There were loud grown-up voices, saying things like 'What?' and 'Where?' and 'Can't be!' Then there were a lot of feet shuffling down the hall. Sarah and Penny lay still. They could tell that all the people were crowding in the doorway, looking at them.

'Kids!' said one of the firemen. 'Can't beat 'em, can you?'

'I might,' said Mr Bell; but he didn't sound cross. He sounded tired.

'I owe you chaps something for your trouble,' said Mr May. He sounded tired too. The firemen made soft, rumbling noises, and their feet shuffled away again down the hall.

Sarah and Penny opened their eyes.

Mr and Mrs Bell and Mrs May were still there. They all looked tired.

'Penny's staying the night,' said Sarah. 'Aren't you, Penny?'

'Umph,' grunted Penny. She still couldn't talk much.

'Is she?' said Mrs Bell. 'I thought you were having a fight.'

'It couldn't be helped,' said Sarah. 'It was *our* fight.'

'Fair enough,' said Mr Bell. 'And it's *our* sugar-gum tree. And the next person who climbs it is going to get well and truly spanked.'

'Twice,' added Mrs May.

'Three times,' said Mr May, coming back down the hall.

'That seems fair enough, too,' said Mrs Bell. 'But I promised Penny no one would be cross if she came down. Do you think this time we might just feed them and shut them up in Sarah's room till morning?'

'Well . . .' said Mr and Mrs May, thinking it over; and the grown-ups went away to talk about it.

Sarah and Penny stayed in bed. It seemed safest, and they were tired too. Mr and Mrs May went home, and Mrs Bell brought dinner on a tray. It was hard to manage, with two in one bed.

'You're tipping it up!' cried Penny when
Sarah moved her legs.

'Stop jogging my elbow, Penny,' grum-
bled Sarah.

Later, when the light was out and Sarah nearly asleep, Penny woke her up again.

'Don't jiggle, Penny. What's up?'

'The . . . the Fire Department!' whispered Penny, and pulled the blanket over her head and shook with giggles.

Sarah was surprised, but she had to giggle too. They went on giggling till they fell asleep.

In the morning, after breakfast, Penny went home. Sarah went with her to the gate.

'I'll bring my teaset,' said Penny.

'Good,' said Sarah. She climbed on the gate to watch Penny walk away down the pavement. When Penny was nearly at the corner, Sarah leaned out from the gate and shouted.

'Penny!'

Penny stopped and turned back.

'I'm sorry . . .'

'Oh, no!' cried Penny, and started to run.

'. . . THAT PENNY MAY IS SUCH A GLOOP!' shouted Sarah as fast as she could.

But Penny had turned the corner just in time.

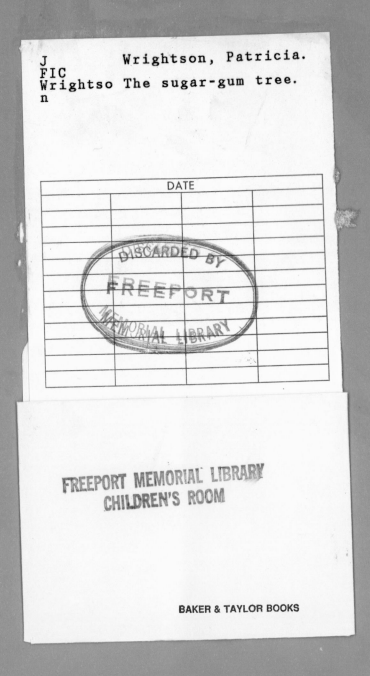